To my aunt Faye Clow, an amazing librarian
who sowed the seeds of curiosity and learning
wherever she went —P.Z.M.

For Alicia —A.W.

Text copyright © 2016 by Pat Zietlow Miller
Jacket art and interior illustrations copyright © 2016 by Anne Wilsdorf

Visit us on the Web! randomhousekids.com

Educators and librarians, for a variety of teaching tools, visit us at RHTeachersLibrarians.com

Library of Congress Cataloging-in-Publication Data
Miller, Pat Zietlow, author.
Sophie's squash go to school/ by Pat Zietlow Miller ; illustrated by Anne Wilsdorf. — First edition.
pages cm
Summary: On her very first day of school, Sophie is reluctant to make friends with the other children,
preferring to play with two squash she grew in her garden—but when a particularly persistent boy named
Steven gives her a packet of seeds as an apology for accidentally ripping her picture, she realizes that it just
takes time to grow a friend.
ISBN 978-0-553-50944-1 (alk. paper) — ISBN 978-0-553-50945-8 (glb : alk. paper)
ISBN 978-0-553-50946-5 (ebook)
1. Bashfulness—Juvenile fiction. 2. Friendship—Juvenile fiction. 3. Seeds—Juvenile fiction. 4. First day of
school—Juvenile fiction. [1. Bashfulness—Fiction. 2. Friendship—Fiction. 3. Seeds—Fiction. 4. First day of
school—Fiction. 5. Schools—Fiction.] I. Wilsdorf, Anne, illustrator. II. Title.
PZ7.M63224Sn 2016
[E]—dc23
2014040340

The text of this book is set in Hoefler.
The illustrations were rendered in watercolor and China ink.

MANUFACTURED IN MALAYSIA
2 4 6 8 10 9 7 5 3 1
First Edition

SOPHIE'S SQUASH GO TO SCHOOL

WRITTEN BY **Pat Zietlow Miller**

ILLUSTRATED BY **Anne Wilsdorf**

schwartz & wade books • new york

On the first day of school, Sophie peeked into her classroom.

Kids were everywhere.
Talking.
Laughing.
Bouncing.

"You'll make lots of friends!" said her mother.

Sophie clutched her backpack. "I won't," she said.

"You'll have tons of fun!" said her father.

But Sophie didn't.

The chairs were uncomfortable.

The milk tasted funny.

And no one appreciated her two
best friends, Bonnie and Baxter.

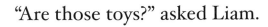

"Are those toys?" asked Liam.

"Do they bounce?" asked Roshni.

"Can we **EAT** them?" asked Noreen.

"No!" said Sophie.
"No, no, no! I grew them
in my garden. They're my
FRIENDS."

And then there was Steven Green.

He sat by Sophie at circle time. Played near Sophie during recess. And watched while Sophie painted.

"Stop breathing on me," Sophie said.

"Steven's just trying to be nice," said Ms. Park.

But Sophie wasn't interested.

So the next time Steven appeared, Sophie bounced Bonnie and Baxter on her knees and said, "I already have friends."

"Me too!" Steven said. He pulled a stuffed frog from behind his back. "I got Marvin when he was a tadpole."

Sophie nodded. "Then you don't need me."

Well, she thought. *That's that.*

But the next day, while she was building
a tower, Steven worked on a puzzle nearby.
　　The day after that, he peered over
Sophie's shoulder when she looked at books.
　　He even chimed in with little-known
facts when it was Sophie's turn
to show-and-share.

Sophie's parents were no help at all.

"Steven sounds adorable," said her mother. "And it's good to have friends."

"Especially human ones," added her father.

Sophie hugged Bonnie and Baxter tightly. "I have all the friends I need."

Still, Sophie knew Bonnie and Baxter wouldn't last forever.

So when Liam showed everyone how to do his loose-tooth dance, Sophie considered joining in.

When Roshni spilled her milk, Sophie almost shared her napkin.

And when Noreen told her favorite banana joke, Sophie laughed—inside her head.

Why are bananas never lonely?

Because they hang out in bunches!

But during recess, Liam, Roshni, and Noreen jumped rope while Sophie played hopscotch with Bonnie and Baxter.

"Can we play too?" asked Steven Green. "Marvin's good at hopping."

"Sorry," said Sophie. "Frogs make Baxter sneeze."

So Steven sat alone.

That weekend, Bonnie and Baxter looked too tired to hop. Or build towers.

"It's time," said Sophie's mother.

Sophie made a garden bed and tucked her squash in for their winter nap.

"Sleep tight," she said. "See you soon."

But spring seemed very far away.

On Monday, Sophie drew squash babies until Ms. Park asked an Interesting Question.

"What makes a good friend?"

"They play with you?" asked Liam.

"They help you?" suggested Roshni.

"They think you're funny?" asked Noreen.

"They like what you like," said Steven Green.

"Great answers!" said Ms. Park. "Let's draw pictures of our friends."

Sophie drew Bonnie and Baxter. She was sprinkling matching glitter when Steven Green appeared.

"Can I see?"

"No," Sophie said. "It's private."

"Please?" Steven tugged the picture.

Sophie tugged back.

Then they tugged at the same time.
Ri-i-i-ip!

Sophie tried not to cry.

"You are **NOT** my friend," she said.

For the rest of the day, Sophie
didn't talk to Steven Green.
She didn't talk to anyone.

Until she saw her mother after school.

"Sweet potato," said Sophie's mother. "That adorable boy didn't mean to tear your picture."

"He is not a good friend," Sophie said. "And neither is his frog."

The next morning, Sophie found
Marvin in her cubby holding an
envelope.

"Hop somewhere else," she said.

And by lunchtime, he had.

When Sophie's father opened her backpack that night,
Marvin and his envelope were inside.

"Sugarplum," he said. "This must be for you."

Sophie opened the envelope. She found a picture of Bonnie and Baxter
and a packet of seeds.

"Do friends really like the same things you like?" she asked her father.

"Sometimes," he said.

"Oh," said Sophie.

She thought for a long time.

Then she took Marvin outside and sat by Bonnie and Baxter.
And thought some more.

As soon as she got to school, Sophie
found Steven Green.

"Your frog had a great idea," she said.

And she whispered in his ear.

During recess, Sophie, Steven,
and Marvin met with Ms. Park.

The next day, Ms. Park gave everyone
a cup, some dirt, and one small seed.

"What are these?" Noreen asked.

"You'll see," Sophie replied.

"Can we **EAT** them?"

"No!" Sophie said.

"You never eat a friend," added Steven.

Soon the seeds were planted in dirt-filled pots.

Steven added water, and Sophie set them in the sun.

"Nothing's happening," said Roshni.

But before too long,
tiny shoots appeared.
Sophie and Steven
did a new-plant dance
and invited everyone
to join in.

"See?" Sophie told Steven. "Sometimes growing a friend just takes time."